Tomie dePaola

STREGA NONA

Takes a Vacation

PUFFIN BOOKS

For Mario, who finally got
a dedication just for himself!

PUFFIN BOOKS
Published by Penguin Group
Penguin Young Readers Group,
345 Hudson Street, New York, New York 10014, U.S.A.
Penguin Books Ltd, 80 Strand, London WC2R ORL, England
Penguin Books Australia Ltd, 250 Camberwell Road, Camberwell, Victoria 3124, Australia
Penguin Books Canada Ltd, 10 Alcorn Avenue, Toronto, Ontario, Canada M4V 3B2
Penguin Books (N.Z.) Ltd, 182-190 Wairau Road, Auckland 10, New Zealand

Penguin Books Ltd, Registered Offices: Harmondsworth, Middlesex, England

First published in the United States of America by G. P. Putnam's Sons,
a division of Penguin Putnam Books for Young Readers, 2000
Published by Puffin Books, a division of Penguin Young Readers Group, 2003

10

Copyright © Tomie dePaola, 2000
All rights reserved

THE LIBRARY OF CONGRESS HAS CATALOGED THE G. P. PUTNAM'S SONS EDITION AS FOLLOWS:
dePaola, Tomie. Strega Nona takes a vacation / Tomie dePaola. p. cm.
Summary: Strega Nona sends home gifts of candy and bubble bath while on vacation,
but when Bambolona grabs the candy, Big Anthony is left with a lot of bubbles.
ISBN: 0-399-23562-0 (hc)
[1. Witches—Fiction. 2. Vacations—Fiction. 3. Bubbles—Fiction.]
I. Title. PZ7.D439Sr 2000 [E]—dc21 99-41362

Puffin Books ISBN 978-0-14-250076-7

Printed in the United States of America

Strega Nona was having *un sogno*—a dream. She was a little girl again in her Grandma Concetta's house at the seashore.

What a wonderful time they were having!

"*Vieni*, Nonalina, *vieni*," Grandma Concetta called. "Come, Nonalina."
Strega Nona woke up. She was in her house on the hill above the little
village in Calabria.

All day long, as Strega Nona helped the villagers with their headaches, toothaches, and other worries, she kept hearing Grandma Concetta's voice from the dream.

Some of the villagers said to each other, "It looks like Strega Nona needs a vacation."

"Big Anthony," Bambalona said. "Strega Nona has something on her mind."

"I know," Big Anthony said. "She almost gave Signore Mayor the wrong remedy for his headache. That's the first time that's ever happened!"

Strega Nona looked out of her window. She was sure that she had heard Grandma Concetta calling to her.

How can that be? Strega Nona thought to herself. *Grandma Concetta has been in* cielo—heaven—*for many years. I wish I knew what the dream meant.*

That very night, Strega Nona got her answer. In another dream she was sitting just outside the little house on the hill. Opposite her was Grandma Concetta.

"Dear Nona," she said. "You've been working so hard all these years. You *must* take *una vacanza*—a vacation. Bambalona can do the daily remedies and Big Anthony can do the chores—feeding the animals, milking the goat, and looking after the house and the garden. My little seashore house is empty, just waiting for you. Come, Nona, come."

Strega Nona woke up.

"*Andrò*," she said. "I'll go!" And she fell back asleep with a big smile on her face.

The next morning she asked Big Anthony and Bambolona to come inside.

"Sit down, my children. I have some news. I'm going to take *una vacanza* at Grandma Concetta's little house by the seashore."

"Oh," said Bambolona. "When will you go?"

"The day after tomorrow," Strega Nona said.

"When will you come back?" Big Anthony asked.

"I will let you know," Strega Nona said. "I will send you a message."

"*Arrivederci*, my children," Strega Nona said. "You'll be fine, Bambolona. If you have any questions about which spells to use, look in the big book. If there are any unusual cases, just go over the mountain and ask Strega Amelia to help you." Strega Nona gave Bambolona *un bacio*—a kiss.

"Now, Big Anthony, I know you'll be a good boy and not get into any trouble. Just do everything you usually do. Help Bambolona if she asks. And remember…"

Bambolona and Big Anthony chimed in:

"DON'T TOUCH THE PASTA POT!"

They all laughed, remembering the day that Big Anthony had flooded the village with pasta!

Strega Nona gave Big Anthony *un bacio* too.

Ah, there it was, the little house at the seashore.

Tomorrow, Strega Nona thought, *I'll send* regali—*presents*—*to* Bambolona and Big Anthony.

The day the presents arrived, Big Anthony was outside feeding the goat.

Bambolona couldn't wait. She opened them and found seashore candy for Big Anthony and bubble bath for her.

I want the candy! Bambolona thought. Quickly she switched the tags.

Big Anthony opened his present. "Bambolona, what *is* bubble bath?"

"You put it in your bathwater and it makes lots of bubbles. It's very nice," Bambolona said, chewing on her candy.

"Oh, no!" the Mayor shouted. "*Non ancora!* NOT AGAIN!"

"At least it's not pasta!" Big Anthony shouted, sailing by on the bubbles.

At the seashore, a dove flew in with a message for Strega Nona. "Bambolona," Strega Nona said to herself. "What have you done?"

"Well, Strega Nona," the Mayor announced, "at least the village will be *molto pulito*—very clean! No real harm done."

"Except when the wrong present gets into the wrong hands," Strega
Nona said. "I hope that YOU have learned your lesson, Bambolona!"

"*Mi dispiace*, Strega Nona, I'm sorry." Bambolona said.

"Me too!" Big Anthony said.

"But Strega Nona, this means that you'll never be able to take a
vacation," the Mayor said.

"*Certo!*" Strega Nona answered. "Oh, yes, I will. Next time, I'll just take Big Anthony and Bambolona with me!"